MISTY meets PALET at SEGERSTROM

Elizabeth Michele Cantine

Illustrated by Sophia Barajas

Designed by Kasey Befeler

www.mascotbooks.com

Misty Meets Palet at Segerstrom

©2023 Elizabeth Michele Cantine. All Rights Reserved. No part of this publication may be reproduced, stored in a retrieval system or transmitted in any form by any means electronic, mechanical, or photocopying, recording or otherwise without the permission of the author.

Photo credits: The publisher would like to thank The Metropolitan Museum of Art for making the paintings shown in this book public domain. Thank you to RMA Photography for the exterior photo of Segerstrom Center for the Arts (cover and page 2), Hugo Schneider CC BY-SA 2.0 for the exterior photo of The Met (page 2), and Markus Spiske through Unsplash for the image of the paint strokes (title page).

For more information, please contact:
Mascot Kids, an imprint of Amplify Publishing Group
620 Herndon Parkway, Suite 320
Herndon, VA 20170
info@mascotbooks.com

Library of Congress Control Number: 2022915896

CPSIA Code: PRT1022A

ISBN-13: 978-1-73211-634-4

Printed in the United States

"Liz, this is utterly beautiful! I love the flow and creativity! Just lovely!"
— **Misty Copeland**

PALET DEDICATES THIS BOOK TO THOSE WHOSE HEARTS ARE
COLORFUL AND BEAUTIFUL

THAT'S YOU

AND YOU

AND **YOU!**

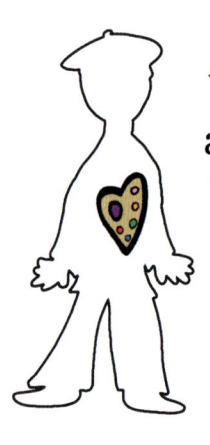

Palet was a painter who wanted to dance. He wanted to dance and pose just as subjects did in famous paintings and sculptures. He hoped to be instructed by a famous ballet dancer—**Misty Copeland**!

After he enjoyed Misty's performance of *The Nutcracker* at **Segerstrom Center for the Arts**, he asked if he could meet her. How thrilled he was to go backstage to talk with her in person! He explained, "I would like to perform at Segerstrom's Children's Festival and in classrooms to share dance and art with all children. Could you please teach me how to dance?"

"Of course," Misty replied. "I love the idea. I would be happy to teach you steps and choreograph a short dance for you! Paintings truly move us all! You could also paint your own picture with the inspiration of famous artwork and from your personal outlook. You could even enroll in a weekly dance class and plan to attend more performances at **Segerstrom**!"

"Great advice, Misty! Thanks, I will seriously think about all this and 'take it to heart.' Plus, I am so happy you agreed to conduct our lessons at The Met in New York, my favorite museum in your home city. I can't wait until next week to see you and to actually dance to some of my favorite works from past artists. I will try to make the past become the present with your help."

Segerstrom Center for the Arts

The Metropolitan Museum of Art

The following week at The Met, they stood in front of an **Edgar Degas** painting, *The Dancing Class.*

Misty said, "This is a good beginning. The students are warming up before class. Look at the dancer at the ballet barre. You can use a chair while doing the movements."

> Hold one hand on the back of a chair.
> With straight legs, reach low then lift to the air.
> Bend slightly back from the upper chest.
> Return upright and long before you rest.
>
> ## PORT DE CORPS

Misty explained, "This is a wonderful, well-known work often hanging in dance studios. Of course, this doesn't resemble ballet classes I take or teach. Why don't you paint one showing today?"

"Yes, I will!" Palet answered. "And I promise to brush in all colors, all genders, all races. Feel the love it embraces!"

The Dancing Class

4

They walked on to **Le Ballet Espagnol** by **Édouard Manet**.

"Let's do character ballet steps to capture the emotion and rhythm of this ethnic dance," Misty advised.

Le Ballet Espagnol

Pose powerful and proud. Hear the loud guitars.
You can point step, point step, snap, snap.
Turn, pose, clap, clap.

TENDUS

Palet was excited. "I'll practice and paint other ethnic dances, too. Look, there's another! It's the **Russian Dancers** by **Degas**."

Misty instructed,

> Lift one leg up, bend at the knee.
> Put it down as the other comes up rapidly.
> One arm up, the other at the waist with energy.
> Eight times, breathe, be strong.
> Though it may look a bit wrong.

EN BOÎTE

Palet was happy. "I really like these moves! I also admire the enthusiasm of the dancers. Although in my painting, I definitely will show more diversity. All colors, all genders, all races dance the love it embraces."

Russian Dancers

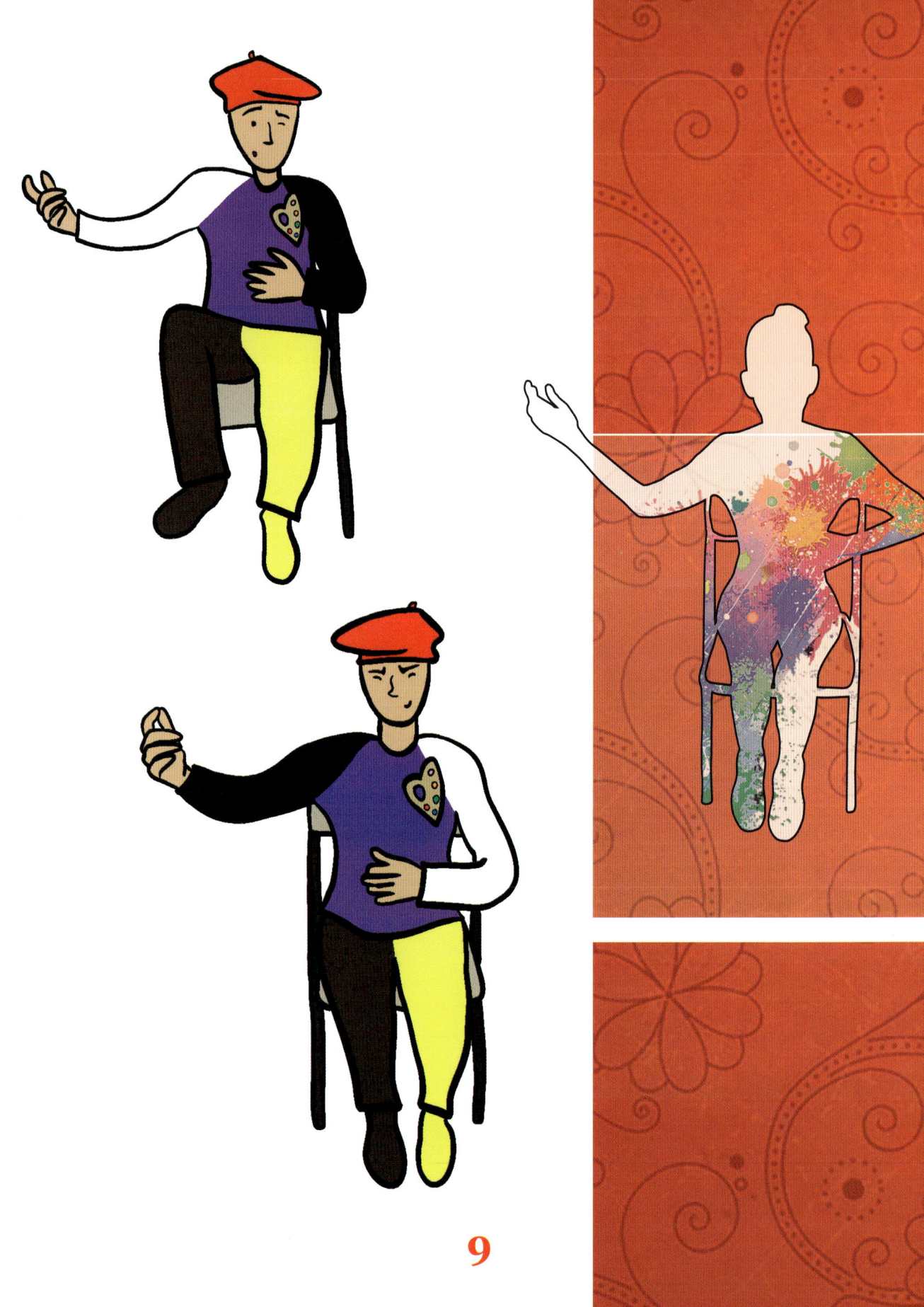

"Since I also like to sing, I selected *The Spanish Singer* by **Manet**. I would like to express his emotions through motions in my dance somehow. I realize many singers move and dance while they perform."

Misty reflected,

The Spanish Singer

It looks as though you can.

Sit on a chair or bench.

Play a pretend guitar you can clench.

Right leg up, put it down, ready to keep beat on the floor.

Then lift both heels up and down which make your feet soar and sore!

RELEVÉ

Palet assessed, "I truly appreciate this Manet masterpiece! However, in my painting, I will show a band with several musicians of all colors, all genders, all races. Hear the love it embraces!"

"That painting looks interesting. I can put on my dancing shoes!" Palet exclaimed as they strolled to **Shoes** by **Vincent van Gogh**.

Misty contemplated,

> **Those could be anyone's shoes.**
> **You can imagine performing hip hop or blues.**
> **Native American, African, Brazilian, here are some cues**
> **Street dancing like they do on a city street or town.**
> **Push it out, be cool, reach low and down.**
>
> ## LUNGE

Palet concluded, "How perfect that the arts are for everyone. It's a language we can all understand! Art, music, dance, and drama can bring us and keep us together with all colors, all genders, all races. Realize the love it embraces."

Shoes

12

The Horse Fair

13

Palet explained, "I love animals, especially horses for their strength, caring hearts, and beauty. I chose **The Horse Fair** by **Rosa Bonheur** as our next painting. Horses can move majestically and sometimes with a constant beat."

Misty replied,

> So stand on the left foot, touch your right foot to the left knee and extend.
>
> It should go straight after the bend.
>
> Then put it down, reverse, and prance.
>
> The audience will surely give it more than a glance!

PAS DE CHEVAL

Palet sighed, "That's a difficult step, but I am going to practice! Someday I will paint my horse show with people riding, admiring, and hugging the horses. Reciprocal love—most animals seem to accept and connect with everyone, just as we should."

Palet continued, "And most everyone enjoys the outdoors. Next, I selected **In the Meadow** by **Auguste Renoir**."

"Oh, Renoir usually paints with soft appearances and airy gracefulness," Misty observed.

> **You can lift long and stretch, seated on the ground.
> Reach out to touch something, keep your arms round.
> Then make shapes with your arms, pick a four-leaf clover.
> Extend and scoop as you bend over.**
>
> ## PORT DE BRAS

Palet pondered, "I like the friendship feeling. In my picture I will also portray two friends at a picnic or at a park with warm hearts and 'cool' personalities! All colors, all genders, all races bond in the love it embraces."

In the Meadow

The Little Fourteen-Year-Old Dancer

Palet dreamily declared, "Ah, it's going to be a meaningful dance. I just need my final pose. I'm certain this **Degas** sculpture of *The Little Fourteen-Year-Old Dancer* will be the perfect ending."

"Yes, I agree," Misty replied.

Start with heels together, toes out.

Then move your right foot so your right heel is in front of your left big toe.

Arms down, hands together, resting behind your back, that's the pose!

FOURTH POSITION

Palet concluded,

"A meaningful ending you suggest.

You've taught me well and put me to the test.

I will honor you and my parents, who model inclusion and diversi

I will fill my new dance, *Paintings Move Me*, with exciting choreography.

I will work on my future paintings with passion and quick paces.

All colors, all genders, all races can see the love it embraces!

Misty congratulated, "I am proud of you, Palet, so continue to paint color into the world with your heart of love!"

Palet gratefully acknowledged, "Thank you, Misty. I'm so happy we first met at Segerstrom and now at The Met! We *will* meet again . . ."

When We First Met

I knew when I first observed the petite twelve year old trying out for Dana Middle School Drill Team Captain that she would become the one in a million as a truly exceptional dancer.

Just from the way she stood, just as a dancer would—perfect poise, presence, posture, and passion. Even then, she was engaged and engaging! I pointed to her and told the former drill team coaches, "I'll take that one!" They informed me that her name was Misty Copeland, and the rest is history . . .

We worked together during the summer to expand her dance vocabulary and to prepare for the upcoming classes and competitions. Amazingly, she learned steps and phrases quickly with excellent execution and perfect musicality. During our first performance in the Dana Middle School Holiday Program, the audience and I were enthralled with her technique and artistry. After that, I made a phone call which eventually led to her first ballet class at the Boys and Girls Club of San Pedro, to San Pedro City Ballet, to South Bay Ballet (Lauridsen Ballet Centre), to American Ballet Theatre (ABT), to her debut as their first Black lead in *Swan Lake*, and then as the first Black Principal at ABT, to her most recent performance of *The Nutcracker* at the Segerstrom Center for the Arts. Misty has danced every step directly and daringly to make a difference in the culture of classical ballet.

Acknowledgments ♡

My Lebanese-American parents who appreciated art, supported my dance dream, and welcomed everyone into our home.

My husband, Richard, who does everything to help me.

My son, Tom, daughter-in-law, Miranda, and grandchildren, Sophie, Aidan, and Maya who offered suggestions and edits.

Our goddaughter, Misty Copeland, who gave me positive feedback and encouragement.

Misty's husband, Olu Evans, who suggested a helpful legal reference.

UCLA friends Mike, author, and Wendy Befeler, for their literary advice and referring Kasey to me.

First cousin Sandra Henry for referring Sophia to me.

Young cousins Layla, Clara, and Bea for their enthusiasm about Misty and dance!

Kasey Befeler, graphic artist, and Dennis Befeler, whose creative talents assisted in the completion of this book.

Sophia Barajas, illustrator, who made Palet real.

Michelle Yamakawa, my college assistant, for her technical expertise and research.

American University of Beirut, Lebanon, where I studied my junior year and learned to appreciate and admire religious, ethnic, and cultural diversity in an institution of four thousand students from fifty-eight foreign countries.

All school districts who implement Arts Education into their daily curriculum and value Dance Education and Physical Education (PE) Dance classes.

The Metropolitan Museum of Art for connecting humanity through art.

Final thanks to Segerstrom Center for the Arts and Studio D for enriching life at all levels.

Meet the...

Author

Elizabeth (Liz) Michele Cantine saw *Swan Lake* when she was four and decided she wanted to become a dancer. That same year she started kindergarten and decided she wanted to become a teacher. She never thought she could do both, but it happened! She began her study of dance with Burch Mann. Years later she joined Mann's professional American Folk Ballet and performed at the opening of Frontierland at Disneyland and at the Hollywood Bowl. While at UCLA, she majored in history and dance before becoming a classroom and dance educator and mentor. She developed teaching units integrating the arts and poetry into daily K-12 curriculum. She also founded a dance program for young adults with special needs called Ready, Willing and Able (RWA). She continues to teach dance to children and adults of all ages. The reciprocal teaching and learning she shares with her students is inspiring, rewarding, and life changing! She is grateful for the talents and colors they give so generously.

Designer

Kasey Befeler is trained in graphic design with a background in concept development, brand identity, and marketing. She enjoys challenges and learning something new every day. In her spare time, she enjoys home renovation, interior design, and spending time with her family and pets. She is passionate about design and finds inspiration everywhere!

Illustrator

Sophia Barajas is an aspiring actress and designer. She is currently completing her final semester at Cypress College where she is earning advanced degrees in theatre arts and dance, as well as certificates in musical theatre and graphic design. She has loved illustrating the character Palet and hopes you love him as much as she does!

You Might Also Enjoy Reading...

Brush of Giftedness

Brush of Giftedness is a collaborative book of original poetry and painted artistic interpretations of famous art. The creatively-formatted poetry is composed by arts educator Elizabeth Michele Cantine, and the artwork is by Heidi Dong, a gifted young woman with autism, an RWA dancer, and Ms. Liz's ballet student. The main goals of this unique book are to expand knowledge about world-acclaimed art and to integrate art, poetry, and dance. It also reminds us that those with autism, Down syndrome, and other challenges do not need to vocalize—the arts validate their volumes of verses. This book highlights the gifts and geniuses of past and present artists. *Brush of Giftedness* is for those who recognize, appreciate, and inspire the giftedness in themselves and others. It is available on Amazon, as is Liz's first book **Graceful Gratitude**.

The Mystique of Misty

From the very first stance
I knew you were destined to dance
At age 12 trying out for Dance Drill Team Captain
In awe of just the way you stood
A dancer's alignment and aura you understood!
She's "the one in a million"—you could, you would!

(Misty's most recent dance performance was at Segerstrom Center, 2019)

Liz can be reached via email at **dancinliz@aol.com**

Paintings in the Book

The Dancing Class by Edgar Degas (page 4)

Le Ballet Espagnol by Édouard Manet (page 6)

Russian Dancers by Edgar Degas (page 8)

The Spanish Singer by Édouard Manet (page 10)

Shoes by Vincent van Gogh (page 12)

The Horse Fair by Rosa Bonheur (page 13)

In the Meadow by Auguste Renoir (page 16)

The Little Fourteen-Year-Old Dancer by Edgar Degas (page 17)

Dance Pose Definitions

Port de Corps: carriage of the body (page 3)

Tendus: tight or stretched (page 6)

En Boîte: refers to a box (page 7)

élève: rise to the balls of your feet or toes (page 10)

Lunge: thrust leading foot forward with knee bent, back leg straight (page 11)

Pas de Cheval: step of the horse (page 14)

Port de Bras: carriage of the arms (page 15)

Fourth Position: one of the five ballet positions (page 18)